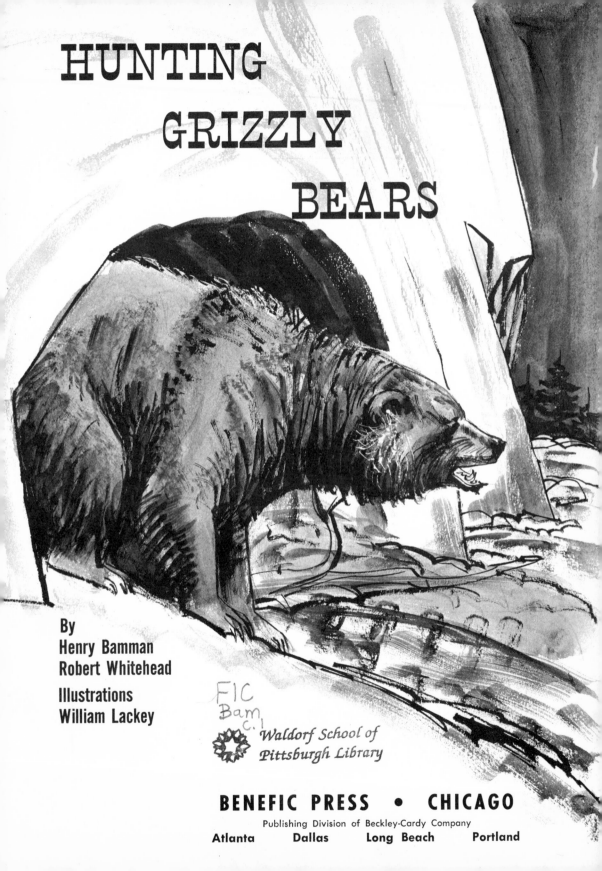

HUNTING
GRIZZLY
BEARS

By
Henry Bamman
Robert Whitehead

Illustrations
William Lackey

BENEFIC PRESS • CHICAGO

Publishing Division of Beckley-Cardy Company
Atlanta   Dallas   Long Beach   Portland

WHY? WHAT? WHERE?

Mark and Rich, along with an Indian boy, track grizzly bears living in the Rocky Mountains.

WORLD OF ADVENTURE SERIES

The Lost Uranium Mine

Flight to the South Pole

Hunting Grizzly Bears

Fire on the Mountain

City Beneath the Sea

The Search for Piranha

Sacred Well of Sacrifice

Viking Treasure

Library of Congress
Number 63-15508

Contents

Silver Tip Gets Away

There was a roar from the dark cave.

"Look out, Rich!" Mark called out to him excitedly. "Here she comes!"

Mark's light caught the head of a grizzly bear in the mouth of the cave. The bear's angry mouth snapped from side to side as she let out a deep growl. She stood up, pawing at the light in her eyes.

The grizzly suddenly came tearing out of the mouth of the cave. Running hard, she came crashing through the brush, right at Rich.

"Fire, Rich!" came Mark's call.

CRACK!

A rifle snapped and a dart of fire thundered through the black night. Whump! It caught the bear right behind the head.

Rich dropped his rifle and picked up his flashlight, turning it on the big animal. He could see the bear in the light. She just stood there in the clearing, a hurt look on her face.

Suddenly, down she went, falling on her back in the meadow.

"Got her!" Rich called out.

"Good shot, Rich!" Mark called to him across the dark clearing.

"Move in, but watch out for her," Rich called.

Mark moved slowly toward the clearing. In the light from his flashlight he could see the dart in the bear's neck. In the head of the dart was a drug to make the bear sleep.

As soon as he was sure that the grizzly was sleeping, Mark would put a tag on her ear. This was the way the two men would mark many of the grizzly bears that were in this country.

There were not many grizzlies left, and Mark and Rich had been asked to help find out all they could about these bears. By doing this, ways could be found to keep the grizzlies the country still had.

Suddenly, Mark stopped. He stood very still.

"Did the grizzly move?" he thought, looking at the bear. "No, how could she move? There is the dart with the drug in it, right in her neck."

Mark moved closer to the big she-bear and then suddenly, to his surprise, she turned over. Angrily she pawed at the dart in her neck, growling and pulling at it with her mouth.

"Get back, Mark!" came Rich's call. "The dart's coming out."

The dart fell from the bear's neck. The grizzly jumped up and turned toward Mark, growling and snapping at him.

"Run for it, Mark!" came Rich's call again.

Just as it looked as if the grizzly would go tearing into Mark, she turned and ran toward the trees. Mark turned his flashlight on her as she ran. Just then his light went out!

The night was suddenly very black. Mark waited there in the dark, listening to the big grizzly as she went crashing through the woods. She did not stop, but ran on and on.

Then all was still. Mark stood listening, but the woods were very dark and very still. Only the wind could be heard in the branches of the trees. The grizzly bear was gone.

"Mark!" Rich called out to him. "Mark! Are you all right?"

Mark called back, "I think so!"

Mark did not look like a hunter of grizzly bears. He was a young man, with clear eyes and a dark face—a man who liked to laugh.

Mark was well-liked—as a man and as a hunter. He was a crack shot with a rifle, and he knew the ways of grizzly bears, too.

Mark picked up his flashlight and clicked it on and off. A point of light brushed against the dark trees over his head.

"Now it works," he said to himself.

"No night hunts for us again," said Rich as he walked into the light with the rifle. "Boy, I thought that grizzly had you!"

Rich was a big man, as young as Mark, but he stood almost a head over his friend. His face was lined by the mountain wind.

Mark pointed his light into Rich's eyes. "By the way, old friend, where were you and your rifle while that grizzly bear and I were going around and around out here?" he said.

"I put the rifle down after that first shot," said Rich. "Then when I went to pick it up, I could not find it."

"Some hunter you are!" laughed Mark.

"But what a rifle this is," said Rich. "Man!"

"Well, the rifle worked all right," said Mark, "but our drug didn't put that grizzly to sleep. From the looks of it, we can't slow down a butterfly with these drugs we have."

"That did it!" Rich said. "Just as soon as Black Feather gets back to camp with those new drugs he went after, we are going right out and let you hunt butterflies with a rifle."

"Good," laughed Mark, "but you had better tell the butterflies I'm coming. You know that I'm a very good shot."

While the two men had been talking, the wind had come up, and now a light rain began falling in the clearing where they stood.

"Let's get out of here," said Rich. "I don't want to get caught out on a night like this with grizzlies running around."

"Why not?" asked Mark. "I thought you said you liked grizzlies."

"I like grizzlies, but grizzlies don't like me," said Rich. "I'm sure they think I'm something good to eat."

"Good to eat? You, good to eat? How could they think that?"

"Come on," Rich laughed. "Let's go!"

"We will have some exciting news to tell Black Feather," said Mark, as he and Rich walked back into the trees. "Our angry grizzly friend at the cave must have been Silver Tip, that big she-bear he was telling us about."

Black Feather was an Indian boy who helped Mark and Rich around the camp. He was going to help the men hunt down the grizzlies and tag them.

"And we let her get away!" said Rich.

"But not for long," said Mark. "I think I know where to look for her and the other grizzlies now. They will not be too hard to find."

"Where do you think they are?" asked Rich.

"The Thunder Mountains!" said Mark. "We have hunted through all the big meadows and caves down here and have seen only one grizzly. The bears must be some place. The Thunder Mountains could be it."

"Grizzly bears in the Thunder Mountains!" said Rich. "Sounds exciting."

"Listen, Rich, it sure will be exciting if you drop your rifle like you. . ."

"Stop! Stop! I give up!" laughed Rich.

"All right, then," said Mark, "but just watch it or some grizzly is going to have something 'Rich' to eat."

"Oh, man," laughed Rich.

By now the rain fell very hard through the trees. The two men walked faster, moved along by the thought of coming face to face with another grizzly in the woods.

The camp was not far away, and it was not long before the men saw the light from their fire through the trees. As they came nearer, they could see Black Feather standing in the clearing. He was calling something to them, but through the wind and rain they could not make out what it was.

They could see Clown, the black bear cub that Black Feather had found, running around and around the clearing, jumping up and down excitedly.

"Something's up!" said Rich.

"Come on!" Mark said.

The two hunters broke into a run and went crashing through the brush toward camp.   (1249)

The Night Camp

"I saw her! I saw her!" Black Feather called out excitedly to his friends.

"Who?" asked Rich as he and Mark ran into the night camp.

"Silver Tip! She was here. In our camp!" said the Indian boy. "Look!"

As Mark and Rich looked about the camp, it was clear that "something" had been there. One end of their boat had been caved in, and running along one side of it were two, new, deep cracks. There were tree branches here and there about the camp. Cans of food were all over the camp, too.

Clown was tearing around the camp, running this way and that. He stopped now and then to nose about the fire.

As Mark and Rich looked closer, they saw what the cub was growling and sniffing about. There, close to the fire, were the big paw marks of a grizzly bear!

"Well, we thought we had some exciting news to tell you, Black Feather," said Rich to the Indian, "but it looks as if our 'news' got here before we did."

"Rich downed Silver Tip up by the caves," Mark said, "but the dart dropped out and the drug didn't work on her."

Black Feather was not listening to the men. "Boy!" he said. "I have been after that old grizzly for a long time. She walked right into camp and I. . . I. . . just stood there. I could not move!"

"Don't give up," Mark said. "Rich and I think Silver Tip and the other grizzlies are up in the Thunder Mountains. Just take a look here," he said, as he pointed down at the paw marks near the fire. "They go off among the trees over there. I could be way off, but I'm sure they will take us to the Thunder Mountains and to Silver Tip."

The Indian boy looked closer at the paw marks. Then he walked over to the tree line, with Clown running along behind him.

"You are right!" he said to Mark as he turned back toward the fire. "Come on! Let's go after her before she gets too far away."

18

The rain had stopped falling by now, but the men could still hear thunder from the mountains. Mark looked at his watch.

"The night is about gone," he said. "I think we had better wait for morning."

"I don't like to hunt grizzlies at night," said Rich, "so I'm with you on that, Mark."

Black Feather was not so sure, but he had to go along with what Mark and Rich said. He eyed the woods again as if he thought Silver Tip was still there. Then he helped his two friends pick up things around the camp.

After a time, Black Feather said to his friends, "By the way, while I was getting the new drugs, I picked up a radio, too."

"A radio?" said Mark. A surprised look came across his face.

"That's right," said the Indian. "A radio. They want us to try and fasten it on one of the grizzlies. Wait here. I will get it for you."

Black Feather walked over to the boat and pulled out a black can. Turning back to the two men, he opened the can and took out a tiny radio only as big as a man's watch.

"Here it is," he said.

"What is this other thing?" Mark asked as he took something from the can and turned it over to look at it. "It sure is light."

"That's the radio finder," said the Indian.

"Well, that's something!" said Rich. "How do they work, Black Feather?"

"When we trap our first grizzly and put him to sleep, we fasten the radio on his ear," said Black Feather. "Then we turn it on right here. See?" The Indian turned on the timer at the back of the tiny radio. "Listen!" he said.

The two men listened, but there was no sound.

"I don't hear a thing," Rich said.

"That's just the point," said Black Feather. "The bear can't hear it, but this radio finder can."

Black Feather took the tiny radio finder from Mark and snapped it on Rich's ear. "Now listen," he said, turning up the timer on the back of the radio.

Rich began to laugh. "Now I hear it!" he said. "Boy, that's something!"

"When the bear runs off, he will take us right to the other bears," said Black Feather.

"How about that!" said Rich.

"I will tell you what," said Mark, as he took the radio finder from Rich's ear and put it to his ear. "Let's try this on Clown in the morning and see if it works as well on a bear's ear as it did on 'Big-eared Rich.' How about it, Clown?"

But the bear cub was running about the clearing, growling and pawing at a night butterfly, and he did not hear Mark.

"All right, you two," growled Rich, with a laugh. "Let's get some sleep."

It was not long before the hunters found a place to sleep under the boat which they had turned over. But for some time, Clown nosed about the camp on the end of his chain. Now and then he put his nose to the wind, growling and sniffing the night air.

After a while, he, too, dropped down close to the fire, put his paws over his nose, and went to sleep.

(902)

Clown Is Lost

The hunters were up with the first light of morning that came down through the trees. After eating, they looked their rifles over closely. They put some of the new drugs into the heads of the darts.

"There!" said Rich, as he dropped a dart into his rifle. "That will stop a grizzly."

"Before we go, Black Feather," Mark said, "put this radio on Clown's ear. Let's see if it is working all right."

Mark took out the tiny radio, and with the help of Black Feather, fastened it on Clown's left ear. The cub pulled at his ear with his paw, but the radio did not come off.

"Turn it on!" said Mark. He picked up the radio finder and fastened it to his ear.

Black Feather pulled on Clown's chain and the bear cub suddenly stopped running about. "Stand still, Clown!" he said. The Indian turned on the timer at the back of the radio.

"There it is!" Mark said. "The sound is coming in very well."

"Then just let Clown keep the thing on," said Rich. "That way we can try it out on the trail."

Mark looked around the camp. "It's time to go," he said. "Rich, the boat is light, so you and Black Feather can carry it. We will have to have it when we get to the river."

"But what about the food and rifles?" asked Rich. "How are you going to carry all that and work the radio finder, too, Mark?"

"Well. . ." said Mark. "I can carry the rifles and work the finder all right, but the food. . ."

"I know what to do," Black Feather said. He pulled Clown over to the boat and fastened the big cans of food to a light chain around the cub's back. Then he put another light chain around the cub's neck and fastened it to himself.

"Don't let go of that chain, Black Feather," said Rich. "If Clown runs off, our food runs off with him. Then what will we do?"

"Food!" Mark laughed. "Is that all you can think about, Rich?"

"But I do think now and then," Rich laughed.

"Good! Then let's think about those grizzlies," Mark said. "Come on, let's go."

Mark picked up the rifles and headed into the trees across the clearing. With Rich at one end of the boat and Black Feather at the other, the two men picked it up and placed it over their heads. They walked into the woods and soon caught up with Mark. Clown ran along behind Black Feather.

For a long time, the hunters walked on through woods and meadows marked by the rain of the night before. It was fall. The trees still had many leaves. Now and then they stopped along the trail to watch the tiny animals running here and there among the tall trees.

From the clearings, the men could see the Thunder Mountains still far off. The dark, black faces of the mountains were very old ones. They were some of the Rocky Mountain chain. These mountains had killed many hunters who were suddenly trapped out in the open by angry winds and falling trees.

The morning was about gone and the mountains still far off when the hunters came out from among the trees that lined a big meadow. Mark stopped and put down the three rifles.

"Boy, those mountains are a long way off," he said. "Let's stop for a while."

"It's about time," said Rich. "I don't know about you, Black Feather, but I. . ."

Suddenly, there was a thunder-like roar from the trees right behind them. Rich jumped. When he did, he dropped his end of the boat. The boat fell over Black Feather's head, slowly pulling him down. Mark turned so fast that he crashed right into the rifles. Down they went!

"Grizzly!" Mark called out.

She was a big one! She was standing back in the trees, just to the right of the men. She rocked from side to side, her mouth opening and closing angrily, her long paws tearing at the air. A deep growl was the only sound she made.

"Mark! The rifles!" Rich called out.

Then, before Mark could pick up a rifle, Rich ran and took a chain from around the boat. Turning, he headed right for the big grizzly, snapping the chain over his head as he ran.

By this time, Clown, who had broken his chain when Black Feather fell, was growling and running this way and that about the meadow. When Clown saw Rich running toward the big grizzly, he darted out after her, too.

The cub ran right by Rich as if Rich were standing still. He went running across the meadow, headed right for the big animal.

When the big grizzly saw all this, the fire suddenly went out of her eyes. She put her head down, and with one last look, turned and ran back into the woods. Clown went running right after her.

"Stop, Clown!" called Mark.

"Come back here!" Black Feather called after him.

But if the cub heard, he did not stop. He ran on into the trees after the big she-bear. In no time, the brush had closed about him.

Rich stopped near the tree line and stood listening. He could hear the two animals crashing through the woods. Then, suddenly, all was still.

Clown was gone. (909)

The She-Bear's Cub

For some time, the hunters stood in the meadow and tried to pick up some sound of the two bears. But only the sound of the wind came back to them.

"Well, let's try the radio finder," said Mark. "After all, we do want to see if the finder works when a bear runs off."

"And Clown did run off!" Rich said. "Man, I didn't know he could run that fast."

"He was lighter when he did not have to carry all your food, Rich," laughed Mark.

Mark got out the can he had put the radio finder in. Fastening the radio finder to his ear, he turned it on. "It's working!" he said. "It's a good clear sound, so Clown can't be too far off."

"Good!" said Black Feather. "I want that cub."

With Mark first, and Rich and Black Feather again carrying the boat, the hunters headed into the woods looking for Clown.

As they moved on through the woods and up toward the mountains, the big trees began to keep out the light. The men stopped only to eat. Then they went on. As time went by, the woods turned dark and still. The only sound that they heard was a crack of thunder from the mountains.

Rich and Black Feather walked behind Mark along the dark trail. They almost fell over him when he suddenly stopped.

"Be still!" said Mark. "I heard something."

It was very dark now, with almost no light at all coming through the leaves of the trees. The night was very still. The men could hear the sound of water as it ran over rocks. Rich and Black Feather put the boat down. The three men stood in the dark, just listening.

"What is it, Mark?" asked Rich. "I don't hear. . ."

"Listen! There it is again!" said Mark. "It sounds like the far-off growl of. . .of a bear!"

"Look! Over there!" said Rich. "In those trees. There is an open place like a meadow."

"Come on, then," said Mark. "Let's take a look. But be as still as you can. And here! Take your rifles. It could be Clown or that big grizzly!"

Very slowly, the hunters worked their way through the trees toward the clearing. Not wanting to make Clown run off if he was there, the men did not turn on their flashlights, but picked their way along in the dark over rocks and around trees. Nearer and nearer they came to the clearing.

Suddenly the men stopped. Something was out there in the night. They could feel it.

Mark turned on his flashlight and pointed it out into the dark night. He moved the light along the tree line, and then across the meadow. There the light came to stop on a fast running trail of water at the far side of the clearing.

"What is it?" asked Rich.

"The Black Bear River!" said Mark.

"Come on," said Black Feather. "Clown could be down there."

Mark clicked off his light and took the radio finder from his left ear. Then slowly he and the others walked into the meadow, keeping their rifles up. They stopped now and then and listened for the sound of a bear.

Near the end of the meadow, the men stopped and looked down at the river. The black water ran like a long chain in the night light. Here and there branches and bark nosed along, exciting the water.

Mark climbed down to take a closer look at the river, but he saw no Clown. He had just turned back to the others when. . .

SNAP!

Rich and Black Feather turned as one! On went their lights!

Then they saw it! Just back from the river, under the branches of some big trees, was a cave. Standing in the mouth of the cave was a she-bear. A tiny black and silver cub nosed about her. The tiny cub did not sniff the three men, but the she-bear did.

The big grizzly let out a deep growl!

"Our grizzly!" Rich said.

"Now we know why she was so angry when we came on her in the woods," said Mark as he came running up. "That cub!"

Rich picked up a rifle and ran closer to the cave. With Black Feather's light on the bears, Rich could see them against the dark of the back of the cave. The she-bear turned to face Rich, keeping the cub by her side.

Slowly Rich took aim at the big grizzly's neck. CRACK!

A dart shot from the end of his rifle!

The cub jumped!

Rich looked up just in time to see the cub's mouth fall open. His shot had gone right by the grizzly. It had crashed into the back of the cub's neck.

"Oh, no!" Rich heard Mark call across the clearing.

The men watched as the cub began tearing at his neck with his mouth. He almost fell over the she-bear as she brushed him with her paw.

"Keep an eye on that she-bear, Rich!" Mark called.

Rich dropped another dart into the rifle. Growling angrily, the big grizzly turned away from her cub and stood up. With fire in her eyes, she looked right at Rich, her nose sniffing the wind. Angrily, her mouth flew open.

Suddenly, though, she dropped down and ran from the cave, away from Rich and her cub. Running hard, she headed for the river. The cub ran after her.

Mark's light caught the big grizzly as she came to the river. She took one look back, and then jumped into the water.

But the cub, running to try and keep up, could only just stand. He rocked from side to side. Just as he came to the river, he fell. Head first, he fell right into the river.

"The cub. . ." Mark heard Rich call out.

But what Rich said after that, Mark was not sure, for he was running as fast as he could toward the river. He got there just in time to see the cub's head go under the water. He waited, but the cub's head did not come up.

The cub was gone, down in the deep river!

(1044)

Trapped

Rich dropped his rifle and ran down to the river. By the time he got there, Mark had jumped into the water after the bear cub.

"There he is!" Rich called out, as he pointed his light down river.

Rich could just see the bear's head. In some way, his head had caught in the brush along the side of the river. Then the cub's head went under again.

Mark got to him just in time. He took the cub by the neck and pulled him out of the water.

"Did you get him out in time?" asked Black Feather, who had come running down to the river. He, too, dropped his rifle.

"I think he is all right," said Mark as he watched the cub closely. He got down over the cub and pulled on the dart. Out it came!

Suddenly, there was a sound from the dark woods behind them. The men jumped as if they had been shot! Black Feather quickly flashed his light across the river. He caught the face of the grizzly as she came out of the brush along the river.

"Oh, oh!" said Black Feather. "That she-bear is coming back!"

"Let me take a shot at her," said Mark.

"All right, Mark, let me get the. . ." Black Feather began. Then he suddenly stopped talking. Mark and Rich looked at him.

"Oh, no!" said Black Feather. "I left the rifle down by the river!"

"So did I!" Rich said.

"What!" said Mark, angrily. "Didn't I tell you. . .?"

Black Feather began to back away into the dark night. "Let's get out of here!" he said.

Mark stopped him. "No! We have to get those rifles," he said. "Black Feather, you wait here. Rich, come with me. We have to try to get to the river before that she-bear gets here."

With that, Mark broke into a hard run down toward the river. Rich came running after him.

By now, the grizzly was across the river. She came up out of the river with water running off her head and down her neck. Growling angrily, she stopped and watched the men closely. Then she let out a roar, and ran toward them.

Mark and Rich were caught by surprise. They stopped still, knowing now that they could not get to the rifles in time. They were trapped! There was only one thing left to do!

"Run for it!" Mark called out.

The two hunters, now the hunted, turned and ran for the trees. Running hard, they could hear the grizzly bearing down on them. On she came, faster and faster.

Suddenly, something came tearing out of the brush right before the men's eyes. It ran right toward them. Mark just had time to get his light up to see. . .

Clown!

The cub ran right by them, headed for the grizzly. The men could hear her growl excitedly as she brushed by them in the dark.

Mark got his light around in time to see the cub go crashing into the big grizzly. The she-bear was surprised, but as she fell back, she shot a paw out at the cub. Clown jumped back.

Around and around the grizzly the cub ran, in and out, pulling and pawing at the she-bear, but keeping away from her snapping paws. The she-bear did not know what to do about the growling cub.

Mark saw the grizzly turn her back to them. "Now!" he said. "Let's get out of here!"

The two men turned and ran. (586)

45

Treed

The hunters ran on and on with the tree branches tearing at their faces. Mark and Rich ran fast, but Black Feather ran faster. He ran so fast that very soon Mark and Rich fell behind.

It was dark and the men could not see well. Rich suddenly crashed into something hard in the dark woods. Down he went!

Mark, right behind him, stopped. He had to laugh when he turned on his light. There, in the hunters' boat, were Rich and Black Feather.

Black Feather had been running so hard to get away from the grizzly that he had not seen the boat they had left in the woods. He had run right into it, and Rich had crashed into him.

"I thought he was a grizzly," said Black Feather as he looked at Rich.

"He is big, all right," Mark laughed, "but not that big, Black Feather!"

Then he laughed again. "Growl for us, Rich!" Rich let out a grizzly-like roar that rocked the dark woods.

"Sounds all right," said Mark, "but. . ."—he looked at Rich closely—"your nose is too long."

"Well, then, help me up, Mark," said Rich. He pulled himself up with Mark's help.

"What do we do now?" asked the Indian as he got up. "Here we are—no rifles, and no Clown!"

"But Clown sure helped us out," said Mark. "If he had not come out of the brush to fight that she-bear when he did, we would not be here now."

"Where do you think he was all that time?" asked Black Feather.

"I don't know," Mark began, "but. . ." He stopped and turned to Rich. "Rich, what did I tell you about keeping those rifles near all the time?" he said.

"I know better," Rich said. His eyes dropped. "But. . .well. . .you know. . ."

Mark looked at his friend. Then he said, "Well, we can't go back with that grizzly still there. Let's get some sleep and then go after our food and other things in the morning."

Mark turned the boat over so they could sleep under it, and snapped off his light. Rich just stood there.

The men were up soon after morning broke over
the mountains. They left their boat under some
branches near the clearing and began to wind their
way back toward the river. As they neared an open,
tree-lined meadow, they heard a sound.

"Listen!. . ." Black Feather began. Then he stopped
and turned his head to one side.

There it was again! Bears growling!

The men worked their way up to the clearing. The
hunters slowly pulled back the long grass that lined
the meadow and looked in.

"Clown!" said Black Feather, excitedly.

He almost called out when Rich said, "Wait! Look over there!"

Rich pointed to two other young bear cubs in the long grass. There was a big she-bear in the meadow, too, brushing her back slowly against the bark of a big tree.

The men turned back to watch the cubs. It looked as if they were taking turns as "it" in tag. While one stood near a tree, the other two would dart in, crack him on the head with their paws, and then jump back, growling excitedly. When the cub fell, the other two would jump on him, growling into his ear. Clown played like one of the grizzlies.

The old she-bear was not keeping a close watch on her cubs. The men wanted to call out to Clown, but they had no rifles. And the big bear was a grizzly.

"Clown gets around. . ." Black Feather began.

Suddenly, there was a sound behind them. All three men jumped!

Turning fast, they saw another grizzly near them. She was a big one with a silver-brushed head and neck. She moved through the trees very slowly, eating the blackberries she saw along the way.

"Get down!" said Mark.

The men dropped down behind some brush. They did not move. They knew that if just the branches moved, the grizzly would see it; she was that close.

"We have to get out of here!" said the Indian.

"Not now!" said Mark. "There is no place to go. Just keep as still as you can."

Now the cubs were up to something. Rich could just see them over the long grass. They were standing still. Their black noses sniffed the air.

"Man!" sniffed the cubs' noses.

The cubs dropped down. Growling excitedly, they darted across the meadow, away from the men. The she-bear looked up when she saw the cubs runnning. She got up, surprised at the growling. Sniffing the air, she turned and ran for the trees across the meadow. The cubs were close behind her.

Rich watched them go. He wanted to laugh at the way the cubs rocked as they ran.

Suddenly a branch broke under Rich's foot. The big, silver-headed grizzly bear heard it and looked up, surprised. Her eyes flew open and a deep growl caught in the back of her mouth. She let out an angry roar and stood up, pawing the air.

Suddenly, the grizzly darted toward the three men, crashing through the brush.

Mark looked up at the tree branches over his head. There was no time to be lost. "The trees, men," he called out. "Climb the nearest tree—fast!"   (807)

The Fight

"Are you. . .all. . .right?" Mark called through the branches of a tree.

"So far so good," Black Feather said.

It had been a fast climb up the tree, and they had made it just in time. As Mark looked down, the grizzly snapped off a branch right under him with her paw. She was so close he could see right down into her mouth. But she could not get to him, for grizzly bears do not climb trees.

The grizzly moved from tree to tree, from man to man, angrily tearing at the bark with her paws. Her head and neck were marked with silver as were the ends of her ears. And she was big!

"It is Silver Tip," Black Feather said.

Here was Silver Tip just a head and nose away, and the hunters could not do a thing about it!

"I don't know about you two," Mark called, "but I'm not going down there right now."

Just as Mark said that, Silver Tip stopped still. Standing up, she pointed her nose into the wind. She was looking across the meadow.

"What is it?" asked Rich.

"Look!" called Black Feather. "Over there! By that open place!"

Pulling back the branches around them, the men could just see into a deep woods across the meadow. There, coming out from among the trees, was a bull. He was a big animal. His big, black head moved slowly up and down as he made his way along.

That is what Silver Tip saw!

Very slowly Silver Tip began to make her way out from among the trees and into the meadow.

As the men watched, Silver Tip moved close to the bull, and then stopped. She took a long look at the bull. Then she fell on her back in the grass and began pawing the air.

The bull could not see well. But he stopped eating and looked up, sniffing the air. Then, he saw the paws going up and down in the long grass. He waited. He looked again. He had to see what those paws were. Then the bull ran across the meadow.

Suddenly, Silver Tip growled and jumped up, right before the bull.

The bull stopped, surprised. A grizzly! He saw he was trapped!

The two animals stood watching one another. Now it was kill or be killed. The fight was on—to the very end!

Up and down the meadow the two animals ran, the bear snapping out time and time again with her paws. The bull carried the fight to the bear, running toward her. Silver Tip jumped away from the bull's angry head.

The end came soon. Going in hard and fast, Silver Tip crashed a paw into the bull's neck. The bull fell, turned over on his back, and was still. It was all over!

Silver Tip was not marked. She nosed about the bull, pawing her kill. Then she fell on it. She did not look around at the hunters. She had found something good to eat.

Mark saw what they must do. "Black Feather," he called out. "Wait here. Keep an eye on Silver Tip. Rich and I will try to get to the rifles at the river. If Silver Tip leaves, go after her. Mark the trail. We will find you."

Slowly he and Rich climbed down the tree, keeping their eyes on Silver Tip. They worked their way around the meadow, going down wind from the bear. The bear did not see them.

When they could not see Silver Tip, they broke into a run. The river was not far. When they came to it, they found the rifles right where they had been dropped the night before.

"Come on!" said Rich.

"Right behind you," Mark said. "This time we have Silver Tip right where we want her."

The men picked up their rifles and walked back into the woods.　(653)

Tagged

The tree branches moved.

"Mark! It's a grizzly!" Rich called.

Something was coming through the woods, right toward the men. They snapped their rifles up in place.

"Don't shoot!" the men heard Black Feather call out. "Grizzlies! Many. . . many grizzlies. . .back there. . .with Silver Tip!"

"It's a good thing you came to tell us, Black Feather," said Mark. "We could have gone back to the meadow and walked right into them."

"What do we do now?" asked Rich.

Mark thought. Then he said, "Well, we sure can't tag all of the grizzlies now. But if we can tag Silver Tip, I think some of the fight will go out of all of them. Let's get back there and see if we can run off the others for now and tag Silver Tip."

"Sounds good to me," said Rich. "Let's try it."

On their way back to the clearing, the men stopped to drop food off near the boat. Then they went on to find the grizzlies.

Just before coming to the meadow, Mark stopped. "Black Feather, you and I can go in at them from this side," he said. "Rich, take your rifle and work your way around in back of the bears on the other side of the clearing. When you are in place, we will call out. Then we will close in. All right?"

"Got it," said Rich. Going off to the left, he broke into a run and was gone.

Slowly, Mark and Black Feather made their way up to the tree line. They wanted Rich to have time to get into place. Pulling back the long grass that lined the meadow, they looked in.

"Look at them!" said Mark.

Grizzlies! There were grizzlies all over. Some were standing about eating blackberries. Others hunted in the meadow, looking for young grasses to eat. All about were cubs, running this way and that, pawing and growling at butterflies. Some of the cubs were playing tag.

"How many?" asked Black Feather.

"I don't know," said Mark. "But. . .keep down!" He pointed across the meadow. "Look! That's Silver Tip over near the bull she killed. When we go in, head right for her!"

It was exciting now. Mark looked at his rifle again and dropped in a new dart. The dart fell into place with a click.

The trees in the woods were suddenly very still. The only sound was the growling of the cubs. The branches over their heads did not move at all.

"Well," said Mark. "This is it!"

Slowly, Mark stood up, pulling his rifle up to his side. He looked around at Black Feather. Then he looked at the bears.

"Now, Rich," he called out.

Mark and Black Feather went running out from among the trees and into the meadow. They headed right for Silver Tip. Running fast, they called out, "Hi-yah! Hi-yah!"

Across the meadow, they could see Rich bearing down on the grizzlies, his rifle up.

Surprised, the grizzlies looked up.

Man!

That was all, but they had seen all they wanted to see. All of the bears ran toward the woods.

But one grizzly did not run—Silver Tip. Standing up, she let out an angry roar that rocked the meadow. There was fire in her eyes as she angrily snapped her head from side to side. The others had left but Silver Tip was going to fight!

Mark and Black Feather stopped. So did Rich. They dropped down in the grass and took aim at the grizzly.

CRACK!

The thunder of rifle fire broke against the trees. Two darts roared into the side of Silver Tip's neck. Another crashed into her back. The grizzly fell back, rocked by the darts.

"Got her!" Black Feather called.

Suddenly, the fire went out of Silver Tip's eyes. Her paws dropped. She rocked from side to side. Her head dropped, nodding right, then left. Then she fell over, right on her face. She did not move. Silver Tip was down—and out!

The men turned the grizzly over on her back. Mark got out one of the tags. Working fast, he fastened it on Silver Tip's left ear. While he worked on her, the big grizzly's mouth began to open and close slowly. Her head began to nod again. She tried to fight her way up from her drugged sleep.

"Watch out!" Rich called to Mark.

The grizzly, in her sleep, shot out a paw that brushed Mark's ear.

The hunters jumped back, their rifles up. They aimed them right at the grizzly.

Silver Tip moved. She turned over very slowly, then got up. Then she fell again, helpless, on her back. She tried again and made it. The men moved back away from her.

Silver Tip took one long, hard look at the men. A growl was deep in her mouth. Then she turned and ran from them, toward the woods. When she came to the trees, she stopped and looked back. She stood looking at the men who had tagged her.

The light coming through the branches of the trees fell on the tag on her ear. The men looked at it. Silver Tip had been tagged!

The big grizzly let out a roar, turned, and was gone among the trees.

The men picked up their rifles and walked toward the trees. Far off, over the trees, in the morning light, they could see the dark, hard faces of the Thunder Mountains. Away off in the woods, they thought they heard the growl of a grizzly. They listened, but there was no sound. All was still.

Vocabulary

The total vocabulary of this book is 287 words. Of these, 267 are below third grade and are not listed; 15 are third grade and appear below in roman type; 5 are above third grade and appear below in italic type. The numbers indicate the page on which the word first appears.

aim 38	dart 6	*rifle* 6
blackberry 51	*drug* 7	shot 6
bull 55	flashlight 6	tag 7
chain 23	*grizzly* 5	thundered 6
click 10	growl 5	
crashing 5	nearest 53	trail 25
cub 15	nod 66	trap 21

* The number in parentheses on the last page of each chapter indicates the total number of words in that chapter. The number underlined on the last page of the story indicates the total number of words in the entire story.

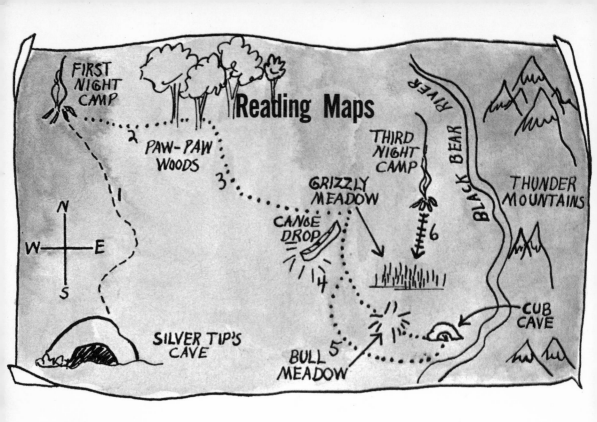

Reading Maps

TRAIL KEY

1 Silver Tip Trail   4 River Trail
2 First Day Trail   5 Rifle Trail
3 Lost Clown Trail   6 Grizzly Meadow Trail

The night after Silver Tip was tagged, the men camped along the Black Bear River near Grizzly Meadow. They wanted to tag more grizzlies. The next morning they made a map of the trails and the country close by to help them find the bears.

"Mark," said Rich, "I think the grizzlies stopped at Bull Meadow after we ran them off. Why don't I follow Trail 4 and come up on the meadow from the south? You can work your way down through Grizzly Meadow on the north."

70

Mark looked at the map and then at the tops of the trees. "The wind is from the south. Those grizzlies' noses would pick you up right away.

"It would be better if you moved southeast on Trail 4. I will come by way of Trail 6 and Grizzly Meadow. Then we can run the bears toward Cub Cave. I don't want to have to follow them to Paw-Paw Woods or Silver Tip's Cave."

"Sounds good!" said Rich. "Let's try it."

News Story

1,000 POUND GRIZZLY BEAR TAGGED

Big Bear—DPI—Two hunters yesterday tagged a 1,000 pound grizzly bear near the Black Bear River.

The two hunters and an Indian boy were on a trip to the Thunder Mountains to tag the grizzly bears that are left in our country. It is thought that about 500 bears are left.

The men were using a new gas-fired rifle with the drug Sucostrin. After the drug is put into the head of the dart, a gas is put into the back of the dart. The dart is then dropped into the rifle. Another gas in the rifle fires the gun.

The men said that as soon as the dart hits the animal, the drug begins to work. Then the dart drops out.

The hunters said that it took about 4 minutes for Sucostrin to put the bear, known as Silver Tip, into a drugged sleep. The bear was unable to move for about 15 minutes.

The men said that the tagging is done while the bear is asleep. The blue and yellow tag is snapped on the ear of the animal.

The men have now tagged 15 bears. They hope to find more grizzlies near Big Bear and the Black Bear River.

"Tall Tales" of Silver Tip

From the time the first men came to our country, hunters have been telling "tall tales" about Silver Tip. These are stories hunters tell to make Silver Tip sound more exciting than she is. As you read this story about Silver Tip, see if you can find the things that make it a "tall tale."

No one knows how old Silver Tip is. Some men say that she began hunting in the Rocky Mountains when time began.

One time Silver Tip called all the grizzlies to the Thunder Mountains to play tag. Silver Tip jumped up and down so hard and fast on the mountain top that she pushed it down and made it a valley.

The Indians say that when it is thundering in the mountains, Silver Tip is growling angrily at the other bears. When water is hard to find, they say Silver Tip has been there to drink.

One time an Indian was boating on the river when Silver Tip took a long, deep drink of water. Man, boat, and all were suddenly pulled toward the grizzly's mouth. The Indian got away when he jumped up and caught the branch of a tree over his head. By then, the boat was in Silver Tip's mouth, and the river was almost dry.

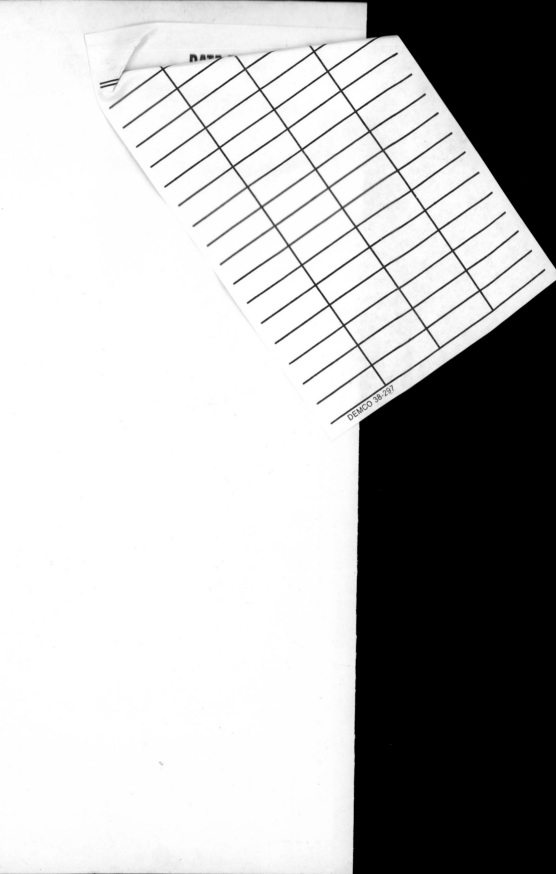